class 3 book Swap

Ernehale Junior School
Derwent Crescent, Arnold, Nottingham, NG5 6TA
Tel: 0115 956 8008 Fax: 0115 956 8006
E Mail: office@ernehale-jun.notts.sch.uk

Copyright © 1986 Victoria House Publishing Ltd
Illustrations © 1986 Martspress Ltd
First published in Great Britain 1986 by Blackie and Son Ltd

British Library Cataloguing in Publication Data
Hayes, Barbara
  Up, Up and Away.—(A Town and Country
  Mouse Story)
  I. Title II. Mendoza, Phillip III. Series
  813′.54[J]   PZ7

ISBN 0 216 92031 0

Blackie and Son Limited
7 Leicester Place
London WC2H 7BP

Printed in Belgium

Up, Up and Away

Barbara Hayes
Illustrated by Phillip Mendoza

Blackie

" 'Allo, 'allo Flora!"

"Someone's calling you, Flora," said Fred one sunny morning.

"How odd," said Flora, looking round. "I can't see anyone."

" 'Allo, Flora, 'allo," called the voice again. It was coming from the sky!

"Why! It's a beautiful balloon!" cried Flora. "And that's Pierre, my French cousin."

Slowly the balloon sank to the ground, and out jumped Pierre.

"Flora!" he cried, hugging her. "Do you like my new balloon? We can go to Paris together. And Annabel and Jeremy must come too!"

What a surprise Annabel and Jeremy had when a letter from Flora arrived by special messenger.

"Quick!" gasped Annabel. "We must pack. We're going to Paris!"

In no time at all they were ready.

"We're off to Paris!" Annabel called to the neighbours as they left. She loved to show off.

"Faster, faster!" shouted Annabel as Jeremy's car whizzed along the road towards Flora's house. "I can't wait to see Pierre's magnificent balloon!"

Pierre's balloon was the wonder of the countryside. All Flora's friends came to see it, and poor Flora was kept busy finding enough food and drink for everybody.

"We will start as soon as Annabel and Jeremy get here," mumbled Pierre through a mouthful of Flora's delicious cherry cake. He was on his fifth slice when Annabel and Jeremy arrived.

"Oh dear," said Annabel, looking at the balloon. "That's a very small basket, isn't it? I'm sure Flora and Fred won't want to squeeze in there."

"Nonsense!" cried Pierre. "There's plenty of room for everyone. Come on, let's go!"

Soon the five friends were drifting over the green fields of France.

"Ooh!" squealed Annabel. "There's Paris — and the Eiffel Tower."

Fred gave a loud sigh. "I hate big towns," he said.

"Oh Fred, you'll have a wonderful time," said Annabel. "Just look at all these lovely shops. Where do we land?"

"Over there," said Pierre. "You can just see the roof of my little farm house."

"Oh good, a farm!" said Fred happily.

That evening they all sat down to a delicious supper. "Why, it's almost like home," smiled Flora.

Annabel sniffed loudly. "I thought we were going to Paris," she said.

"Do not worry, Annabel," said Pierre. "Tomorrow we will all go sightseeing."

The next day they drove into Paris and saw all the famous sights. Flora was so excited that she waved at everybody — even the policemen.

Annabel and Jeremy decided to go to Paris every day and, of course, Annabel bought lots and lots of clothes.

Jeremy took Annabel to the races, so she could show off her newest dress.

"You look as pretty as a picture," Jeremy told her.

"You're right!" she exclaimed. "So I do!" And in no time at all she was posing for one of the most famous portrait painters in Paris.

"I'll hang it in the hall at home," she thought to herself, "so it will be the first thing everyone sees when they come to visit."

Flora and Fred enjoyed themselves walking in the countryside near Pierre's little farm.

"Who would have guessed that French fields are just like our own!" Flora said happily.

One day they went to a country fair. Even though she spoke only a little French, Flora decided to have her fortune told.

"It was very exciting," she told Fred afterwards, at the hoopla stall. "The fortune-teller said I would win some gold!"

"And so you have!" laughed Fred as Flora's ring flew through the air and dropped neatly over a big bowl of goldfish!

At last the time came for them to go home. Pierre drove them to the harbour and sadly waved goodbye.

That evening, Annabel was back in her own bedroom again, trying on her new Paris hat.

"I must go to Paris again soon," she murmured. "And next time I will remember to take some bigger suitcases!"

"Oh look!" said Flora, when she and Fred arrived home. "I've forgotten to post all our postcards!"

"Never mind," said Fred. "We'll send them from here. They'll look just the same."

"Didn't we have fun in France," said Flora, as she looked at the postcards one last time.

"Yes," said Fred. "But isn't it nice to be home!"